Dear Matthew!

I hope you enjoy the book and tell your friends about it.

Wish you good luck with your career. xx

19/10/12

Dream Vs. Destiny

A single True Story based on the
Experiences of many Afghans

Written by:

ARIAN POPALYAR

authorHOUSE®

AuthorHouse™ UK Ltd.
500 Avebury Boulevard
Central Milton Keynes, MK9 2BE
www.authorhouse.co.uk
Phone: 08001974150

First published by AuthorHouse 11/5/2010

ISBN: 978-1-4520-7824-3 (sc)

This book is printed on acid-free paper.

Editor: Elizabeth Eyre
Cover page designer: Fareeha Naz

Author's Acknowledgement

Afghanistan was known as Europe of Asia and then the war destroyed it, I want to dedicate my book to Afghanistan and to all I love: my Allah All Mighty, father Zia Ahmad Popalyar, Mother Shukrya Popalyar, best friend Maria Vega, Neelam, my Popalyar family and to all my cousins, my London Met group of friends, friends from L.K Bennett and my other friends whose prayers are always with me, Elizabeth Eyre without you it was impossible thanks for everything.

Author's Biography

Arian Popalyar is young energetic Afghan girl whose family faced different problems in afghan war they fled to Pakistan, she grew up watching many afghan families fighting the battle of life in Afghanistan and then as refugee. Being a sensitive person she use to telling stories in school, her friends loved her stories asked her to write but she ignored saying life is long to do that but the earth quake in Pakistan made her realize that life is too short so after finishing the school she start writing a story then leave it in mid and after the gape of seven months she completed the novel, she is the only child of her parents she is studying software engineering in London Metropolitan University, she is a brave girl who love her country the trouble of her life has made her tough some of her saying are below:

Hard work without vision is fruit less.
Mostly discouragement gives you more
strength to do your best in order to prove
yourself; which makes you successful.

Things that you worry about soon or later they will come to your life but this time will never come back so enjoy it fully.

Contents

Chapter 1

'Run, Ayesha! Run!' said Suzy, but Ayesha said "Suzy relax [1]yaar ([1]buddy)".

"Ok let's go this way. Everyone is in the Oxford auditorium. Can you hear the sound of clapping, Ayesha?" Suzy said.

"Of-course buddy; this is the day I fulfil my dream - where we will be crowned for our four year's of hard work", sais Ayesha. At last they both reached the hall where the announcer was calling the name of Ayesha for the third time:

"Ms. Ayesha Popal, please come to the stage to receive your certificate". She moved toward the stage with great confidence. Her heart was full of joy and her eyes were sparkling with pleasure. She receives her certificate and the hall thunders with the sound of clapping. Suddenly she hears someone calling her name –'Ayesha! Ayesha!' - Her brother Imran beating her on the back - 'Wake up you silly girl! Wake up!' She opened her eyes and saw Imran in front of her and said, 'You stupid boy! Why do you always do this to me? Ooh I was so happy; holding my certificate'. She hit her brother with the prospectus of Oxford University, which she had been clinging to in her sleep. Imran says: "Stop! Silly girl, you and your dreams; since uncle sent you this prospectus you can't see anything else. Don't you know the condition of state is getting worse every single day; so stop dreaming ok? Anyway, you know uncle; he just send this to fool you; he is not going to give you any other help. You know that he is very practical and loves his own money so you'd better stop day dreaming". Ayesha says "Whatever Imran, I trust myself and I know that one day I will achieve my goal, I will show you, and people like you that anything is possible if you have courage". Imran says, "Ok, we will see. But for now go to the kitchen - Mom needs your help".

Ayesha hurries to the kitchen and says: "Salaam Maa (Mother), what are you cooking?" Her mother replies "[1]Qabile Palaw" ([1]famous Afghani dish). Ayesha says "But don't you think it's too early for making dinner? It's only 5 o' clock." Her mother says, "My dear, your brother said that he will be home from work soon, and once he is home you know how hungry he will feel. Besides this the fighting may start again today and then things will get even worse, so let's stop talking and start working, come on". Ayesha says "Ok Maa". Eventually all the food is prepared. Ayesha says "Maa its 6:30pm where is [2]Padar ([2]Dad) and brother?" Mother says, "I'm worried too my dear. After the fighting it is only their second day of being back at work. I'm so worried, from the time they leave in the morning until the time they come back I feel like I am on fire." Ayesha says, "I know Maa,' suddenly there is

2

a knock on the door. Ayesha says 'It's them –wow- super timing.' She opens the door and say, "Salaam Padar Jan (greetings dear father), how are you?" Father says "I am fine baby, how are you? Is your brother back home?" She says "Padar Jan, relax, come in; everyone is fine, but brother is not back yet." She closes the door and they hear the sound of firing. Father shouts "Oh no! I guess the fighting has started again. All Mighty Allah please help us! Everybody, heads down and move towards the safe location in the house".

Ayesha and her family used to live in Mecroyan, which is a very famous residential part of Kabul city where people lived in apartments. When they heard the sound of bullets the people from the second, third, fourth and fifth floors rushed down to take shelter in the basement. Those basements were designed to get rid of water from snow. Now the basements were being used as human shelter. The rest of Ayesha's neighbors came downstairs panicking and making a huge amount of noise. But Aeyesha's family didn't go to the basement because they lived on the first floor. After a brief pause of about three minutes the sound of bullets continued. The clock struck 12:00, but still there was no news of Ali; still he hadn't come back, everyone was very worried. Finally, the clock struck 1:30am and the sound of firing stopped. Everybody came out of their hiding places and stood before the door, staring at the door and praying for Ali's safe arrival. At 2:00am someone knocked at the door.

Papa called "Who's there?" There was no answer but instead, a faster knock. Papa finally gathered his courage and opened the door and was surprised to see

Shah (Ayesha's uncle). Shah was clearly frightened and his forehead was sweating, he said "Salaam everyone. Brother, I have decided to leave Afghanistan. Me and my friends have arranged a truck for us to leave for Pakistan tomorrow, I came here to tell you to go with us. Pack what you need quickly and come with us". Papa replied, "No. Never. No way! How can you think like this? I'm not going with you and neither is my family. Come on Shah, this is our country, our motherland, how can we leave like this? I believe things will return to normal". Uncle says "¹Lala (¹Big brother in respect) don't believe nonsense. The condition of the state is very bad and it gets worse day by day". But papa denies uncle gets increasingly angry. To enforce his words he said, heatedly, 'Enough! No more discussion! The state condition is critical and we are leaving." Papa was quiet but Uncle Shah's mood was changing. He became very nervous but then he became relaxed appealed: "Brother listen, I respect you and your patriotism but this is the matter of life or death of our family and for that we can make no compromise. But when he gets no response he says "find but I don't want your patriotism to ruin the life of my daughter so tell Ali to come to our house early in the morning when we are leaving I want him to go with us. Where is Ali?" Papa said, "He is not back yet". Uncle Shah said "What do you mean? Where the hell did he go?" Papa replied "He's been away from work for a whole month because of the war, but yesterday he went to the office because nothing had happened for three days and they told him to come in for his salary. So that's where he went, but he is not back yet and we are waiting for him".

Suddenly there was a deliberate knock at the door. Once again, without knowing who was there, Papa opened the door. Everyone gazed at the man who came in. He was tall and handsome but his face was pale, his forehead sweaty and his eyes darted furiously around the room. Then we recognized him as my brother's best friend who had travelled with him that morning. Father said, "Shamas! So late at night. What has happened? Where is Ali?" The time was 4:00am and no one had slept. Imran shouted "Shamas are you hurt?" He replied "No, I am fine, but".

"Then where does this blood come from?" said Imran. Shamas replied "Actually Actually".

"What? Come on, speak what happened'" Father said with anger shaking him by his arms.

He replied "Ali is injured and he is in hospital". On hearing these words Maa (mother) fainted.

Ayesha tried to support her mother and Imran went to bring water. They threw water over mother who regained consciousness. Shamas continued saying, "We had collected our salaries and we were on the way home when suddenly the suddenly firing started. We were frightened but near home so we just started running, but a bullet caught Ali and he fell down. I somehow managed to drag him to the side of the road. But he was loosing blood; I was scared and desperately started looking for a vehicle. I saw a car and shouted, "Hey! Brother help us! My friend is injured; I need to take him to hospital!" There was no reply, so I ran towards the car and saw that the owner was dead at the wheel. I pushed him out of the vehicle (may All Mighty Allah forgive me, but I had no choice) then I drove Ali to hospital. When we arrived the hospital was full of wounded people. There were few doctors and many patients. I gave two month's pay to the doctor who took Ali to the operation room. I came here to take you all to the hospital, please get ready and go with me".

We all went to the hospital but first Uncle went to his home to fetch his family. When we reached the hospital the scene was horrible, all round you could see wounded people who were crying for help. Some had lost legs and some had lost hands, there were dead bodies and the place smelled unearthly. After seeing all these horrors, we finally we reached the operation room. The red light was on. We waited out side. Everyone was crying and praying. We were told that at least five major operations were taking place in the same room because of lack of space and equipment. All of us kept praying that my brother's operation would be successful.

My brother was engaged to the daughter of my Uncle. Her name was Seema. I can still remember the day of they became engaged as if it were yesterday. It was two years ago when we all went to Paghman with my Uncle's family who had three children: two sons and a daughter. The Paghman District, as it is also referred to, is located at the west of Kabul city. The area is green with plenty of trees and fruits. Located at the bottom of the Hindu Kush, Paghman became a holiday retreat with villas and chalets as well as the summer capital. It was a popular place for wealthy Afghans and the Afghan

aristocracy to visit. It is a place where people relax and spend the weekends with friends and relatives. It is known for its beauty, with many lakes, rivers, and waterfalls. At the entrance is the European style monumental gate, similar to that of the Arc de Triomphe in Paris, but smaller. Kabul River, the only main river in the Kabul Province, is fed by springs and snowmelt runoffs from Paghman. After his 1927 – 1928 tour of Europe, India and Iran, King Amanullah brought in foreign experts to redesign Kabul.

The story behind their engagement is very interesting and it begins in Paghman where we had planed to stay for a week. While going to Paghman we had two jeeps. In one jeep it was all the ¹pacha-party (¹group of youngsters), and the rest of family were in the other jeep. The journey was so lovely, trees at both sides of road and steep hills. Paghman is only 250 km away from Kabul but when we arrived it was dark as we had set out quite late. We had booked rooms in the Paghman Hotel, as we were all so tired and hungry, I think we had used up all our energy during the journey in singing and enjoying ourselves, so after supper everyone went to their rooms to rest. The next morning was very beautiful I woke up earlier than normal days and stood on the balcony to enjoy the pleasant morning. Birds were singing, the wonderful blossom of flower was spread all round, I was immersed in the natural beauty when suddenly I saw my brother. I was surprised to see him so early because usually he would wake up quiet late. He was dressed in jeans and an orange shirt with a denims coat; he was then twenty one years old, a handsome boy with nice a hair cut. Then I saw a girl… It was Seema. She was wearing an orange shirt with white embroidery and a jeans skirt her curly black hair looked beautiful and although her complexion was not that fair but she had striking big black eyes. My brother plucked a flower and placed it in her hair, and then they took each other's hands and started walking. I wasn't that far from them but they didn't realize that I was there because they were so involved with each other. I rushed back for my camera but when I get back they were gone. But I said to myself that from now on "I will keep my eye on them". Seema was nineteen years old and she had finished high school. And my brother was doing his undergraduate degree in engineering. I was so surprised to see them like that- for me it was so unfamiliar to see people acting like that together. They used to behave so strangely in front of everyone else. They were so formal together as though they just cousins. For me my cousins were like brothers and sisters, but this relation was not the brotherhood at all, it was something else which I was yet to find out about. I had always had a very investigative nature and this was like a new assignment for me. I looked at my watch and it was 7:00 am. I went back to my room. Everyone was starting to wake up. I decided not to share what I had seen with anyone. We all went downstairs for breakfast. My brother and Seema were there too, they said "Salaam" politely to each other as though they had met just now for the first time that day ; I kept my eyes on them; my brother's eyes had an amazing shine in them.

We all went hiking. Wow! We were moving across the jungle among thick trees - it was really special, I was taking pictures but my brother Imran was so naughty he snatched my camera and started running with it., I am very possessive about by belongings so I started following him; we were running carelessly and I lost control and fell on Seema and she was hurt badly I somehow managed to look after myself but she fell and was about to fall from the steep mountain but my brother Ali jumped and managed to save her and took her in his arms and carried her to the hotel . When we arrived at the hotel my parents were shocked to see Seema in my brother's arms; Seema's Mom cried "What happened?" and they all took Seema into the room. I thought everything would be alright but when my brother came back he was so angry and his eyes were red and he gazed at me as though he was going to kill me, I got scared, (I'm sure Seema was not as hurt as she was pretending to be I can't walk and bla bla, but there was no one who could make my brother to realize this.) He came directly to me; I was in the hall and everyone else was there too. I gave a stupid smile and said "How is she now?" I had no idea what else to say at that moment, but my brother slapped me so hard that I almost fell on the sofa. My mother shouted "Ali, what's wrong with you?". But he didn't listen he just yelled "You stupid girl, how dare you do this to her! You almost killed my love. You don't know what she is to me, I love her more them my life". Everyone else was listening to his words, even my Uncle. But I could hardly hear anything because   my face was hurting so much, I was crying and my head was ringing I just saw stars but my brother's words were so shocking that no one paid any attention to me. When he finished talking there was a deep silence in the hall, then everyone started laughing, my father was older then my Uncle and he said to my him "So what do you say brother? when should I come to take away my daughter in law?" he was quiet and had no feelings on his face; I thought this would finish only here. Because I didn't like Seema and after the slap I really hated her, but my Uncle answered "anytime, Lala" [2]([2]big brother) and so it was done. Their proposal was *accepted by all the family and the engagement party took in a hotel in Kabul. Everything happened unimaginably fast. After that day we went back to Kabul and the engagement party was two weeks later. Then we just had to book the hotel, buy the dress and distribute the invitation cards, and do a dozen little things to prepare, but at last everything was done. I worked really hard but with an unwilling heart. I was my parents' only daughter and they loved me a lot, which made me obstinate by nature sometimes. I didn't say a single word to my brother because I was angry with him. The evening before the engagement I was upset because my dress was not stitched properly, I was very sad and was standing before the window and looking outside. Everything seemed to be against me then I heard a voice "Ayesha!" I looked back, it was Ali, and I turned back to the window. He called me again and I continued to ignore him but then he came near me and said "My sweet sis is still angry with me. Why baby? Look at me". I kept quiet and didn't turn to him, then he turned me to look at him and said "Sorry". He touched his ears and repeated: "I'm sorry. I will not do that again. I swear, sister please forgive me please, please." Then I smiled and hugged my brother. I really love my big brother, I call him Big B. Papa called him and I was left alone with a gift he had left for me. I opened the gift he had given me, it was a gown. Wow! It was perfect, as I thought it would be. A black gown with silver embroidery. After making peace with my brother I finished my green tea and went outside to join Mom who was busy in preparation for the next day. The whole room was covered with all the necessary goods some packed up and some still to be packed up. Imran was busy packing and Mom was ironing everyone's suits and dresses I sat down to help Imran with the packing. I think we packed about twenty gifts - enough for Uncle's whole family then we turned to packing the goods we bought for Seema: her sandals, her clothes and make up, and all kinds of other things. When Mom finished ironing she went to the other room to bring Seema's jewelry. We placed everything on different trays and decorated them with chocolate, flowers and ribbons. We had our dinner late that night as everyone was so busy. My brother brought barbequed food and cold drinks. It was a very tasty meal, I was so hungry. The real reason the food tasted so good was because my brother, Ali put his whole heart into it. My brother goes after everything with his whole heart that is the sign of true human being. After everything was finished I went to bed at about 1:00am, my Mom didn't get to sleep until 4:00 am. The next day we got ready for the party, which was to be in the evening. Mom went to the beauty parlor with Seema and her mother while I got ready at home. Before leaving for the parlor Mom put rollers in my hair. I wore my dress and silver jewelry, the only make up I added was lipstick as I was not really a make-up person, I usually love wearing jeans. Mom gets back at 3:00pm. Dad and Imran were ready. Papa was wearing his gray suit with a white shirt. My Dad is half bald but he still looked graceful with his suit and glasses. Imran was wearing his black suit with a silver shirt. I got angry because his outfit made him looks like my twin. I guessed Big B had bought him that suit; they were his favourite colours, but I complained to Papa and poor Imran changed his black suit and wore his blue suit instead. Imran is always quite cooperative. Mom was wearing her elegant brown gown and she looked lovely. We were all ready by 5:00pm. I stood at* reception with my cousins Kausar, Hosai, Ogai, Masooda and Benazir to welcome the guests. My cousins gave me lots of compliments about my gown. Finally the party began at 6:30pm and the bride and groom arrived at the hotel at 7:00 pm. Seema was wearing a magenta bridal gown and Ali wore his black suit with a magenta shirt and tie that was Seema's favourite colour, what a sacrifice big b but never mind. They both looked so cute together just as though they were made for each other. There I accepted their relation with full heart and forget the bad past and I enjoyed the party fully. They cut the cake, everybody danced and we had a great blast. My cousins are very nice girls. They all came from different cities of Afghanistan some from Kabul city, some from Qandahar and Mazar-e-Sharif. We had a great time and after taking the bride to her house we came back to home at 2:00 am. But a loud cry from my Mom brought me out of my memories.

My Uncle arrived at the hospital with his family. My mother hugged him them and started weeping. My Uncle's Wife is a very nice lady she is just like a sister to my mother; they were both crying and trying to comfort each other. Seema was also crying but less than I thought she would. I think Seema was in shock her face was pale her; eyes are senseless, her hair disheveled. She was weeping but my Dad tried to console her by saying "Have patience my dear and pray to All Mighty Allah for Ali instead of weeping".

Since I arrived at the hospital I hadn't been crying, I was trying to control myself in front of Mom, but when I found myself out of her sight, I cried a lot.

Our country had been in a state of war for as long time.

But it had just been in the rural areas, no one had any idea that this war could become so drastic and deadly.

We waited for three hours; finally a doctor and a nurse came out. He was about forty year old, a he was a heart specialist. Shamas rushed to doctor and asked, "Doctor how is my friend?" The Doctor recognized Shamas as the boy who brought my brother to hospital and gave him the fee. All our eyes were on the Doctor, full of hope. I was waiting to hear his words, my brother's handsome face was before my eyes and all my attention was on the Doctor. Then he said "the bullet has passed very near to his heart and penetrated his heart, the big vein is broken; without a heart transplant there is no solution and a heart transplant is not possible here, so I'm very sorry to tell you that we cannot save him. His condition is critical and he has only a few minutes to live, you can all come in and see him." When I heard this I thought my heart would give up too. We all rushed into his ward. My All Mighty Allah my brother looked so tired and his eyes had huge dark circles under them, his colour was pale. He just had time to look at all of us and say the holy verse of (kalma Shahadat) and then he closed his eyes. I felt as though the earth had fallen away from my feet everyone started crying, I thought my Father would fall to the ground but my Uncle supported him. Seema was lifeless; like stone she gave no cry she made no sound. I felt like the room was revolving around me my brother's face flashed before my eyes and then everything was black and I couldn't see anything. When I opened my eyes I was in a common ward's bed in hospital Imran was sitting next to my bed and it was the next day, all around were many people crying, and my bed was stained by blood. It wasn't my blood -the bed wasn't clean but that they had found me a bed was enough. I asked Imran "Where is everyone else?" He asked quietly, "How are you feeling, now?" I said "I am fine Imran can I see Big B please". I couldn't stop myself from crying and Imran started crying too. I never saw him cry like that before; he was in twelfth grade, a tall boy of five feet eleven inches. He was looked like an angry young man but his behavior was always very jolly, you can't stop smiling when he is around. But that day in hospital his colour was pale and his eyes had dark circles like he hadn't slept all night and had cried a lot big B was his buddy and during the football games no one could touch the remote they bet and get crazy dad as well all the fun went with him. Imran wiped his eyes and took my hand and said "If you are fine let's go home. Everyone is at the funeral waiting for us".

When we reached home it was packed with people dressed in black and the sound of crying could be heard all along the street. I saw my Papa and hugged him but he remained still he seemed bowed like a defeated king. Mom and Seema were still crying. Then I went to see Big B; I gazed at his face which was shining like the moon. After a while Papa and the other men gathered to take my Big B away. I felt like they were taking my life away. It was so horrible; I never thought war could be that terrible. At that moment I thought things would never be normal again and that nothing could be more horrible than this moment, but then I had no idea that fate had different tests for me yet.

Chapter 2

Thirty days after the death of my beloved brother we heard the news of Seema's marriage. I shouted "What the hell? How can this be possible?" My Mother and Papa heard me and came out. I continued "Imran are you in senses? Who told you about this? How could she think of doing this?" Imran said, "My sister, it is already done, next week Saturday in [2]Peshawar [2](city of Pakistan) ; look at the card, they are going to Pakistan tomorrow Seema's brother gave it to me". I tore the card in anger, my head was burning I didn't know what to do, but my Dad said "Why have you torn up the card? She had to marry someone she can't stay alone all her life. My brother told me about this marriage and I agreed it was a good idea". I rushed to my bed room; I was so upset; my brother had loved her so much and they were about to marry; they were in love, how could she do this? My brother was so madly in love with her that he even don't care about me and that's why he hit me and now he is dead and she won't wait for even a year to pass or even his[1]chilum ([1] the 40th day after the death of any Muslim is called chillum). From that day the meaning of love changed for me. As fate would have it, Seema's marriage happened before fortieth day had elapsed from my brother's death. While we were all crying, she was happily beginning her new life.

The condition of the country was very extreme. I was at home and it was three months since I had seen my school friends. All schools were closed because of the war. After his retirement Papa had invested his money in a medical clinic which and a doctor friend of my father ran. This provided some income monthly and with my Mom's job as well we somehow managed to survive. We had good terms with the doctor's family; they had been a great support to us when my brother was in hospital.

Someone knocked rapidly at door; I opened it was Father. He rushed in, he looked worried and his face was tense I asked, "Papa, what happened, come on, tell me?" I called Imran to bring some water, he brought some and Mom hurried in. I was very eager to know what the matter was; suddenly the firing started and with the firing the heart rending sound of people crying also began. We put out the candles, we were on the first floor so we remained in our house. When the firing started the neighbors all rushed to reach the basement where it was safe. After ten minutes there was silence everyone had stopped struggling to hide; the only sound you could hear were bullets firing from all round. You can never tell if you have become the target. Papa had calmed down and Mom asked "What happened?" Papa replied "We lost our shop." Mom said anxiously "What? When? How?" My brother and I were thinking the same questions. Papa said "This afternoon when I was on my way to the shop and I only fifteen minutes away; I heard the sound of a blast. When I got there, there was a fire in the shop and one wall and the roof were completely destroyed". Mother asked "What about Dr. Zaki? How is he?" Papa said "He is no more; he was in the store, busy working, unaware of his approaching death. When I arrived I found him very seriously injured and he lost his life in my arms". Mother cried, "No My All Mighty Allah". Mom started crying uncontrollably. But Papa said "Come on, hurry, we have to reach to their house, they need us now so come on and get ready". Imran and I also wanted to go with them but Papa said "I have lost one son I don't want to lose you too now. You both stay at home, if we can get back we will leave Afghanistan and if we don't come in twenty four hours you both leave to Pakistan. I have telephoned your aunt Mena". I was crying. Those were really the hardest words I have ever heard. I couldn't imagine my life without my parents. But Papa was insistent and asked Imran to promise to stay. He left saying these words to Imran: "You will not come with us and you will take care of your sister. I hope we will be back". As Mom and Dad left the house, I fell down crying I felt so helpless that day. I never thought life could be so frightening. But when you are not in control of your life what else can you expect from this world?

Chapter 3

One moment the sounds of fighting outside would seem to be slowing, the next the sound of bullets would return even louder than before. I started to say my prayers. I prayed to All Mighty Allah for the safety of my parents. I had no idea where Imran was. I just felt that I was not part of the world. It was a dark night, full of the silence of death. The sound of firing had stopped and I felt relief that at least one horror was over for a while. I prayed that Mom and Dad would arrive safely. Suddenly I heard the sound of ladies shouting nearby: "Please leave me help, help, help. I was very frightened, Imran rushed from his bedroom and said "Ayesha, go and hide yourself somewhere that no one can find you just go inside". I asked "But what is going on, who are these people?" Imran said "This has never happened here before, so I have no idea; but these are the bad people no one knows, which group they belong to, maybe they just want to take advantage of war but they have weapons and they are robbing people; I saw that they caught some of the girls from the other building. We have no weapons at home to fight back; so go". I was so frightened that I hid myself in the cupboard of kitchen behind the drum of rice. The sound I of the women I had heard had been close and the next moment they were outside our door they beating at it violently.

Imran had no idea what to do. If he didn't open the door they would surely break it down so in the end he opened it. They pointed the gun at Imran and said; "Who else is with you? Tell us!" Imran said "I am alone. There is no one here". The man said "Oh really" and then he ordered the others: "check the entire house and take out everything you find." They searched all the rooms while one man remained with Imran pointing the gun at his head. This man was the leader he shouted orders to the other men. One of them went to kitchen.

I could hear the sound of his footsteps. I hold my breath. He was just opening the door of the cupboard where I was hiding when suddenly the man from the hall called. "Hey you; what the hell are you doing out there? No one has cooked Palow (dish made of rice) for you; get the hell out of there you rascal". The man left the kitchen and I took a deep breath. Then I heard the sound of scream and people moving quickly. Then there was silence, I stayed where I was for half an hour because I was so scared. But when I heard no sound from my brother I began to get very worried and I made myself come out and face reality. The faces of Imran and Big-B flashed before my eyes and I put my head in my lap and started weeping , then finally I dared to come out of the cupboard and rushed towards the hall. The whole house was messed up, I was walking but my feet were not moving as fast as I willed them I was taking tiny baby steps until I reached the hall. The door was open and Imran was lying on the floor. I ran to him, he had been hit badly over the head and it was bleeding. I was shocked and I bent my head down to hear his heart beat. The heart was beating. Then I checked his breath and he was breathing. I become so happy I hugged him; then I rushed to fetch some water and threw it over his face. After this he regained consciousness and I went to my bedroom for the first aid box. My All Mighty Allah the bed room was destroyed, it was a horrible mess the cupboard was open with everything in disarray but I ignored everything and got the first aid box and rushed back to the hall where I bandaged Imran's head. Mom and Dad arrived, the door was open so they came straight in and they were shocked to see the bandage on Imran's head and that the whole room looked like world war three had broken out. Mom cried out and they both come forward to support Imran. We took him to his room and he took a pain killer and went to sleep, then we turned to the house. Papa went to check the cupboard for money. Papa had a deposit of two lacks plus Mom's jewelry and some important document but the men had taken everything except those documents. Papa was shocked and Mom was weeping but they were not sad to loose the money instead they were happy that we were alive. That night Papa decided to leave Kabul forever because with each passing day it was becoming more like hell.

The next day Imran and Papa went to hire a vehicle and they managed to get some money by selling the gold chains that Mom and I use to wear daily and which were all we had left after the robbery. But when they came back they said they hadn't been able to hire a car yet but had talked to a truck driver who would come tomorrow to take us away. Then we get relaxed a bit as we realized we had at least got one more night to stay in Afghanistan. Mom and I went to the kitchen to cook some food for lunch. I was quite surprised the food that we had bought to last a month had almost run out. The shops were closed due to the war and things were getting harder bit by bit. Anyway we cooked potatoes for lunch. Then I asked Mom to let me go to Palwasha's house. She was my best friend and they lived very nearby to our home. We had been friends since childhood and had studied in the same school. Papa took me to her home, which was in the next building to us. When I get there the memories of childhood moved before my eyes. The park, which was always crowded with people was empty that day, no one was there and all around was a deep silence even the birds who used to sing melodious songs had vanished. We reached to their house and Papa began to move to ring the bell, but seeing that there was no light, he knocked at the door instead. Palwasha's father opened the door with a blank face. I was surprised, because he was a very jolly person. I couldn't figure out what was wrong, I was just trying to understand his expression. We greeted him but he made no reply suddenly someone started crying from inside "Save her! Help! Leave her leave her aaaahhh". He rushed in with my Papa and me following. It was Palwasha's mother's voice. As you enter Palwasha's room you will find her smiling picture that was taken at her birthday last year. She is a beautiful girl. My eyes were searching for her because she was like my sister, I found her mother in her room hugging her favourite teddy bear that I had given her. Her mother was in a very strange state, she started laughing uncontrollably; there were five ladies trying to calm her down. She was a working woman and had a graceful personality but at that moment she looked very horrible. I become frightened by the absence of Palwasha. I couldn't bare the suspense and felt angry the laugher of her mother and the crying of the ladies penetrated my ears. I put my hands over my ears so that I couldn't hear anymore. Finally Palwasha's mother became unconscious and the sound stopped. The women were looking after her. I asked "Uncle where is Palwasha?" He stared at me with blank eyes and started crying and saying "I could not save her" I was feeling so distressed and desperate for someone to tell me where Palwasha was? My Papa came to comfort Uncle. I saw her brother and said "Tell me what happened? Has Palwasha gone to your elder brother's house? Why is this crowd gathered here"? Then I realized I didn't want to think what the answer might be. He said "Yesterday when those robbers arrived we were bringing water with Palwasha and Papa ...... when they took her Mom and Dad tried hard to stop them but every effort was useless, they had guns with them and they forced her inside the vehicle; then some of them moved on to get new victims, she somehow managed to get out of the vehicle. Mom shouting and she was running towards Mom then those rascals fired three bullets at her and she died on the spot. The funeral was yesterday, many neighbors gathered, your Mom and Dad were there as well to perform the funereal acts. Why have you arrived now?" No one had told me. Now I realized why Mom didn't want me to come here. That whole day was hell; I spent it at home with the memories of my childhood with Palwasha. I was thinking about her all day and feeling so aggressive and angry. Whenever something happens to someone near to my heart I feel so aggressive and sad.

When I first heard the news of Palwasha's tragic death I was sense less for two minutes. I cried a lot. I went back and hugged my Aunt and cried a lot and she cried with me until she fell asleep and we left.

I was backing home at 9:00pm. The next day Dad and Imran went to the bus station and brought a truck for us. We sat in it with our luggage. We had hardly managed to bring anything with us because the truck was already loaded with goods and people. But, there was enough room for us to sit, and the journey started. Luckily the other people on the truck were very kind, they were mainly families and educated. I was seated on luggage and facing backwards. When the vehicle was moving I felt like someone was stealing Kabul city from me. But now the civilization of our city was damaged badly and all the well reputed, educated people were leaving Kabul city and the villagers were now arriving to live in the vacant apartments of city, although many villagers had also left the country a huge number of them had came to cities. Because of this every day in the city one would hear new practical jocks; and on the balconies of the buildings you would find cows and goats.

Three hours passed. We were out of the main city now. We were passing through different areas some rough, some tough. The journey took two days instead of one day because at every check point near Pakistan our truck was stopped unloaded, and then reloaded. All this loading and unloading took about three hours. Plus the speed of this truck was also very slow. I was very tired. Finally we reached Peshawar at 9:00 pm. It was night but the city was lit so it seemed bright and it was wonderful to see light after such a long time. We got our luggage, rented a taxi and went to my Aunt's home. I was so tired and sick from the journey that when I got there I fell asleep almost immediately. They were so happy that we had arrived, they had cooked delicious dishes. I hardly had five bites before I fell asleep again. I kept having the same dream. I dream that I am running in a university campus in the United Kingdom. I wake up when I heard the cry of a girl and the sound of bullets I thought it was Palwasha; I opened my eyes as I was calling her name. Her face flashed before my eyes, I quickly jumped out of bed and ran out of the room to see what was going on. But then I remembered I am not in Kabul, the sound was coming from the adjacent room I rushed in and saw my cousin was watching a movie. I shouted "Turn off the TV!", My head was burning, my face was red it always happened whenever I got angry. When I am angry I become the world's most dangerous person. I called his name and said "Umer, turn off the TV!". He asks "Why what happened? I shouted "Turn the TV off". Then I moved toward Umers as if I were going to eat him. Then I snatched the remote control and switched off the TV and said, "Can't you understand that someone is sleeping in the next room and don't you have anything better to do in the early morning than watch movies? You…"

Umer was the son of Ayesha's aunt. He was three years older then Ayesha and he was a 1st year student at Peshawar university. Her aunt had four children. Two daughters were married and the youngest son was in sixth grade. Ayesha's aunt was married to a Pakistani man; he was the son of the Pakistani Ambassador; who become friends with Ayesha's grandfather during his transfer to the Kabul in Pakistan embassy. After their marriage they started living in Pakistan they used to visit Kabul once each year. It is believed that Mena, (Ayesha's aunt) and Farukh (her Uncle) married for love. Now back to where we left.

Umer said "Relax, relax Ms. Ayesha chill buddy. First of all it's not morning; watch you're your watch it says 11:00 am, which is almost lunch time in Pakistan and for your kind information today is Friday and it's holiday here so I was enjoying myself and one more thing everyone else is awake and busy and last but not least, I admit that the TV was loud but I had it loud knowingly so that you would wake up; I just wanted to make sure your were alive otherwise the way you were asleep it seemed to me that you had no plans to wake up for a week! Any way Asalaam-o-Alaikum (Peace be upon you) and welcome to Pakistan. How are you feeling here out of the bloody country of war?" Ayesha says "Hey don't you dare say a single word about my Afghanistan, ok?". Then she left the room. On returning back to her bedroom she saw the wall clock said 11:30-nearly noon. She noticed the room for the first time – it was big and well furnished with two beds, lots of dolls and soft toys and nice decoration. It had been the room of Mena's daughter. The colour combination of room was pink and white. Ayesha moved toward the big white cupboard; and she found the salwar kameez (Pakistani national dress) of her cousins and under that she found her bag and she put on her pink shirt and jeans and rushed downstairs, and said "Salaam(Peace) [1]khala jan ([1]dear aunt) salaam Maa (mother)". Her aunt replied "Salaam, my dear how are you; I hope that you slept well at night?" she says "Yeah Khala jan I slept well after a long time. I had such a nice sleep". Her aunt gets emotional and says "Oh my dear I can understand." She hugged me and then she started crying because of Ali. Then mom and I also started crying. The death of Big B was a great loss to our family. Suddenly Uncle Farukh comes into the kitchen and says "Meena I am so hungry honey, is the food ready? Ooh what happen why you are all crying?" Uncle was a very nice man. He somehow manages to make us laugh with his broken, broken Dari. Instead of getting emotional he tried to lighten the atmosphere. It's true that when people are sad and crying they need to come out of that sadness and all they need is someone who can make them laugh. I never thought I would laugh again, but Uncle's nature was wonderful. Anyhow, we stayed there for two weeks. Eventually Imran and Papa's were searching for a rental house finally they find one paid off and we packed our luggage. Aunt gave us a stove, blankets, a heater, a fan and kitchen-utensils to help us in our new house. The next morning after breakfast Imran brought a vehicle and we loaded it with all our thing, but when we reached the house; there were already people inside so Imran and Dad went to talk with the owner of house. When they came back Imran was red by anger; Mom asked "what happened?" Papa said "owner of the house has given the house to someone else and he says if we want this house we have to pay triple since these people have given double rent they us". Then we went back to aunty house. We were upset but it's an Dari proverb "yak dar basta sad dar baz" means when one door is close hundred other doors gets open at evening my dad's cousin called from other city of Pakistan and when they come to know about our problem they said they had have rented a big house in Mansehra which could easily accommodate two more families so they said we can go there and we will share the rent. Papa agreed to go to Mansehra. Our luggage was packed so we decided to leave early in the morning for Mansehra. Mansehra was about four hours drive away from Peshawar. As we approached Mansehra, the weather became pleasant. Mansehra is one of the most beautiful cities in Pakistan in terms of natural beauty. The journey was so lovely. At both sides of road there were trees, the mountains were covered with greenery and the trees seemed like green carpets over the mountains. Finally we reached my. She gave us a very warm welcome. We spent the whole day chatting with them. She has one son and a daughter. While chatting her husband my Dad about some good schools that I could go to. Soon I got admission to school. After a month Dad went to Kabul to sell our house as the money that we brought with us had almost run out. He was back in a week life was going well there and soon my dad's cousin family went to Germany. Since their case was under process since one year.

With the money that dad brought he stated a small shop.

The people of Mansehra were very kind and hospitable but also very religious and narrow-minded. One day during break time I was chatting with my best friends about the war in Afghanistan and how modern Afghanistan was before the war. One of my friends was jealous because she came second in everything and I always came first. This meant that she was always trying to humiliate me. She said "yeah it's because the people of Afghanistan were so modern and use to drink and the women wore skirt that is why Allah destroyed it with war." That was also the perspective of older people in this town. But with them I couldn't do anything, but she was really in trouble my blood was boiling and I turned toward her and gave her a tight fisted punch and her nose start bleeding. She was crying and all the girls gathered around us and the teachers came and took her to the hospital. Then the principal called my parents I had to wait in the principal's office my Dad came in and had meeting with principal. Finally the principal said to my dad "Considering the record we have of your daughter's we are not taking any action but if this happens again I will expel your daughter from this school." Dad apologized and things were settle so we left for home.

Papa was very angry but since he loved me a lot and was a professor himself so he just asked me "Tell me what happened?" and I explained the incident. Dad smiled and said "Good." But then changing his tone he said "next time no matter what happens or what anyone says. You will not do or say anything. This is their country so they have the freedom to say or do anything but we are mahajir (migrants). What if they had expelled you today? So you must promise me this will never happen again and you will control your nerves." I said "I promise I will not do it again. But was she right? Was our country destroyed because of modernism? What is Islam all about?" He said "My dear, Islam is the religion of peace and its components are far superior then the skirt or drinking. Tell me if some non believer stops drinking will he become Muslim? I answered "No". Dad said there you are You are Muslim if you believe in Ones of Allah and that Prophet Muhammad (PBHUM) Basically Islam teaches the Oneness of Allah, it teaches us to believe in all the prophets like Adam and Eve, Joseph, Moses, Jesus and the last prophet Muhammad, in the Day of Judgment, in heaven and hell, all the holy books like Bible and the Quran. If a Muslim wears a skirt or drinks alcohol he will be sinful but by doing so he will not become a non-Muslim but neither everyone in Afghanistan wore skirt nor every one use to drink and afar as the destruction of Afghanistan is concerned it is just a massive political game. Once you have the right believes it depends on you that how practicing believer you are and you will be answerable to Allah for all your deeds but one thing is for sure that your religion does not allow you to kill people. Because Allah says in sura Maidah verse number 32 "On account of this We prescribed (this Commandment in the Torah sent down) to the Children of Israel that whoever killed a person (unjustly), except as a punishment for murder or for (spreading) disorder in the land (i.e. punishment for bloodshed and robbery etc.), it would be as if he killed all the people (of society); and whoever (saved him from unjust murder and) made him survive, it would be as if he saved the lives of all the people (of society; i.e. he rescued the collective system of human life)." Now you go to your room and I will go to say my prayers.

Five years passed and Ayesha's family stayed in Pakistan. Ayesha was at college now. Her brother Imran went to Peshawar University to continue his education as there was no university in the small town where they live.

Ayesha had grown and was a tall, fair, beautiful girl who was full of life. She had long black hair and big hazel eyes. She had grown to have a super nature and control of her temper. When ever she was happy she used to dance and also when she got angry she would dance too; strange perhaps… but that was the way Ayesha was. All her friends use to consult Ayesha in times of trouble as she was a very brave girl, ready to face anything. She had been through such a bundle of hardships, which had deleted the word of fear from her dictionary but there were lots of things that she had not experienced yet. Her big hazel eyes were filled with dreams of going abroad to complete her higher education but like other the girls she also had a dream of a prince who would come one day to take her away from her turbulent environment, the one who would resolve all tensions but she had no idea how he would enter her life.

Chapter 4

It was morning and Mother was saying "Ayesha, Ayesha, stop. Finish your breakfast [1]janu ([1]beloved), look your brother has gone far away and now you don't listen to me". Ayesha said "My God! Oh Maa (mother) it's ok. I've already had my breakfast and I am done now. And I don't want to become an elephant ok? Maa, make sure you pray for me as these are the final exams, after them it's all over....ok, I've to go, Mua bye! Dua is ringing the bell I have to rush". She opened the door and saw Dua and Neelam, her best friends. Ayesha said, "Hello; how are you?" Dua replied "Forget hi and hello and rush we are getting late". Ayesha said, "Ooh just a sec buddy let me put on my scarf of mother Teresa style". Then they hurried off and at last they arrived at college. Ayesha said "See we still have fifteen minutes to spare. You were making us hurry for no reason". Neelam says "she is always like this tension box" Dua said, "Ayesha" she replied "Yes". Dua asked "Today is the last exam, no?" Ayesha said "No today is the first exam". Dua got angry and said "Don't joke, I am serious". They say "Yes dear, today is the last exam". Then Dua said "That means we will not be able to meet daily anymore". Ayesha said "Oh my Laila Dua (Laila was the name of a legendary female character in an ancient Asian novel) don't get emotional buddy. So what if it is the last exam, we will keep in touch through the net and I hope that one day you will become my sister in law and we will always be together". When she heard this Dua said "Shut up, Ayesha". But Ayesha continued to tease her: "Why do you feel shy about it? Neelam says "Hey Dua, you've even gone red". Dua said "I will kill you". Ayesha and Neelam started running and shouted "Catch us; hey race you to the examination hall".

The exam was three hours long. Afterwards everyone went back to their homes. When Ayesha got in her father was not back from the shop yet. She went to her bedroom and fell asleep. She was free now, there were just the practical exams left and then she was free for three months.

Ayesha spent the first three months of the holidays doing some embroidery but then she became bored and restless and while sitting alone she said to God "Dear All Mighty Allah what should I do for the next three months?'

At that moment 'Ding Dong' the door bell rang. Her mother called "Ayesha open the door please". She replied 'Ok Maa I'm on my way. Who's there?" "It's me, Imran". She opened the door and said "Hey bro, how are you? What a pleasant surprise." They hugged each other and Ayesha said 'I missed you so much". Imran said "I know,

I know my wild cat, now come on, don't get emotional I am not alone I have brought a friend with me".

Ayesha remembers herself and becomes more alert. Then she said "Ok, ok but wow what a car! You came in this? Who's car is it?" Imran replied "It's my friend's car. Now move aside I am taking the luggage in, but you stay here and show our guest in". Imran went inside and the other guy emerged after parking the car. He was about 5ft 9inch tall, wearing trousers and a shirt; his age was 29; he had Asian features, a normal complexion, big black eyes and his hair were nicely cut. He seemed quite nice and he looked like a decent gentleman.

Ayesha was in the habit of talking to herself in her head. She said to herself "Is it necessary for Imran to always bring some friend with him." Then she turned turns towards the stranger and unconsciously looked into his eyes. He comes directly towards her while staring into her eyes and for the first time in her life she felt butterflies in her stomach.

That day Ayesha was wearing black trousers with a long maroon shirt. Her long black straight hair made look stunning. The man came closer and said "Salaam." Ayesha replied in her normal manner: "Welcome, this way please".

Ayesha took the man into the guest room and soon Imran and her mother joined them. Imran introduced the man to his mother saying "Maa this is my friend Hamza. He did law in England and now he has college in England. We met at my friend's wedding in Peshawar and we become friends. And as he was coming here so we decided to make the journey together. His family lives in Abbottabad," (Abbottabad is a small city near Mansehra) .

Then he turned to Hamza to introduce his mother but he found his friend busy looking at something. Imran said, "Hey Hamza, what are you looking at?" Hamza snapped to attention and said "Nothing; just that embroidery frame". Imran followed his eyes and said "Oh, that frame right behind Ayesha". Hamza said "Yeah" then Imran said, "My sister, Ayesha made that". Hamza said "Oh great". Imran said "Ok Hamza, this is my lovely mother." Hamza said very quietly "And my mother in law". Imran did hear him clearly and said "What/ Pardon?" To cover up Hamza said "I mean, my mother will be worried about me, I must give her a call". Imran said "Ok, go ahead, but first let me introduce my sister to you. This is Ayesha, you met her earlier. My lovely, silly sister. She is crazy about going abroad for her education". Hamza says quietly "And I am crazy about her". Again Imran said "What Hamza?" And Hamza answered: "Ooh my mother will be crazy with worry about me; I have to tell her wear I am". Then Imran said "Ooh ok then make your call first". It seemed that Hamza was also in the habit of speaking with himself. In fact, I think actually all humans have this habit.

Later Imran looked towards Ayesha and made a sign for her to bring tea. Ayesha and her mother brought tea and cookies and they all enjoyed them together. During tea Hamza explained all about himself, he seemed to be a very powerful man, he had been to college in the United Kingdom, he owned property, and he had business in Dubai. Ayesha kept gazing into his eyes. Hamza promised that he would help Imran to get to Dubai and support him so that he could start a business there.

After tea, Hamza left to return to his home. Imran went to sleep, their mother to the kitchen and Ayesha to her room where she stood before the dressing table studying her reflection. She had long, black, straight hair, big, hazel eyes and a white complexion. It occurred to her for the first time that she was beautiful. Then she felt embarrassed and shy about looking at herself in the mirror. When people get tense they often talk with their subconscious. This is what Ayesha did. It happened a great deal of the time with her. She was her own confidante and she believe that no one in the world could love you or know as well as your own self. Your own self can guide you best.

She would also speak to the Lord (and although she didn't receive any direct response she never stopped asking questions because nature do give you answer but in some other way.) "Oh my All Mighty Allah what is going on with me? I feel that my mind and heart are no longer one". It was as though my mind was saying, "Ayesha! Relax he is just a boy, like any other guy and he is not that handsome and he is older then you are just twenty! So wake up!". But it was as though the heart was saying something else: "Ayesha age doesn't matter, buddy. He is so cute and the way he looks at you - he loves you". Mind: "Oh come on Ayesha, how can you say he loves you?" Heart: "Of course he does, can't you see the love in his big eyes? And he is a successful man, what more do you want?" Heart, Mind, Heart, Mind. Ayesha became so confused and irritated that she shouted "Stop it!". Then there was silence. Ayesha said "Ok, ok, whatever it is I need some time. He is successful, he is cute but I don't know anything about his feelings so I had better slow down. I'm sure this can't be love. I am just impressed and that's all, nothing less nothing more and this could just be a mad crush; anyway I need to slow down and give my self some time".

That evening when Ayesha's father came back from the shop all the family sat down together and began to tell him about Hamza. After hearing about Dubai and the promises he made to Imran Papa says "I want to meet Hamza so invite Hamza to dinner tomorrow evening. When I have met this man I can consider whether I will allow Imran to go Dubai or not".

So we invited Hamza for dinner, dinner was the best time as Dad was at home at night. Hamza came to dinner but because he brought some friends with him I was not able to talk with him. He ate dinner with his friends in one room and I remained in the other. After that evening Hamza started coming to our house every week. He also came to my brother's birthday party. But, again we hardly had any chance to talk to each other. He did ask me for my email address and, which I gave him. Now I had the opportunity to talk with him online, I started to spend a lot of time sitting at the computer sending him emails and waiting for him to come online, but he was a very busy man. After a month his visits to our house became far rare. He had to go to Dubai to deal with some important business matters and he become even busier than before. I used to wait for days for a single email. All the time I was dying to hear his voice. I couldn't understand what was wrong with me and then finally I realized that I love him; if a strong girl like me could spend all her time thinking about one person, waiting for one person it could only be love. I finished my practical exams and had two months of freedom ahead of me. So I started working in an organization. (A charitable organization)

One day, Ayesha's best friend, Neelam, come to her house greeted her mother and asked "Aunt, where is Ayesha?" Ayesha's Mother replied "Your friend is asleep in her room go in and wake her." Neelam said "Ok, Auntie."

Neelam went to Ayesha's room and shook her bed shouting playfully: "Ayesha …. Wake up." Ayesha was startled from her sleep and woke crying "Aaaaahhhhh…" and then when she saw her friend she said "Neelam you" She replied "yes me". Ayesha said "Oh you! Damn it why do you always have to take me by surprise when you arrive and scare me and make me jump." Neelam said "Because I want my entrances to be memorable hehehe." Ayesha said: "You scared me. Again. I thought it was an earthquake". Neelam said "Oh come on Ayesha, the earthquake happened on 8th October 2005. Six months have passed now. You didn't die in the earthquake; you won't die in after shocks now." Ayesha said "But you know our shop was badly damaged that cause a financial loss and we need someone else's help in sending Imran to Dubai." Neelam said "I know my dear but listen to me, now you have to do something." Ayesha asked "Why, what has happened?" Neelam explained "Actually Dua called me. She is sick of receiving proposals and her family is ready to give her away." Ayesha was immediately worried and said "What? Oh no." Neelam said, "Oh yes. Now you get ready. We are going to her house, ok?"

We went to Dua's house; things had gotten more serious than I had expected; we stayed for a while chatted with Dua and returned. That evening I discussed the matter with Imran. He said "I have got my tickets to Dubai and soon I will be independent; sister please, you have to do something. I love Dua and I don't want to lose her". Ayesha said "I understand brother. I will do whatever I can because I know the pain of love". So I discussed the issue with Maa and Paa. The next day they went to Dua's house to ask for her hand in marriage. Dua's parents agreed when we told them that Imran was going to Dubai and would soon become independent. We asked for no dowry because in Afghanistan the man is responsible for both sides of the dowry. I was very happy with how things had turned out: this time my sister-in-law was of my choice. We fixed a date for the engagement to take place the very next week. The party took place in the Green Hotel in Abbottabad. As it happened, Hamza was back from Dubai, and he was able to come to the party. We also invited him to bring his family. We had never met any of his family before, this was my first chance to meet them and impress them I was very excited but nervous as well. This time all the preparations went smoothly. Everyone looked their best the bride and groom in particular looked fantastic. Imran was now twenty three years old a handsome young boy dressed for the evening in a black suit and a pink shirt and tie and Dua looked stunning in a shocking pink gown with golden embroidery.

Padar had invested a lot of money in this wonderful

party. From the moment I reached the hotel I couldn't stop myself looking for Hamza and his family. Eventually I caught sight of him standing alone in a corner. I was confused and angry to see that he hadn't brought his family.

I think me and Hamza both knew that we loved each other but we had not expressed our feelings yet; at times we would hint at our feelings in front of each other, but nothing more. Because he was older than me I used to call him "Sir". It was strange. And was it strange that we had not expressed our feelings yet? No! I'm a girl so how could I be first to express my feelings. He should be the one to express his feelings first. I was completely lost in these thoughts when a voice saying my name called me back to reality. It was Hamza's voice. I turned to face him.

"Oh my Barbie doll. You look smashing in that lovely dark blue dress" he said. I wanted to thank him for the compliment but my mind seemed to be stuck and I stood like a statue looking deep into his eyes. Often when he spoke to me I would freeze and even if I did manage to chat to him I would blush. I felt somehow as if when he was around I lost all control of my body. With great effort I managed to say, "Thank you, Sir". Hamza sounded disappointed: "Sir?' Oh please dear don't call me 'Sir', call me Hamza. After all, I love you". Finally it had come, the moment that I had been waiting for so long, I felt like my heart was flying through the air. I felt like I might loose consciousness, I was stunned and although my eyes were open for a while I couldn't see anything except him and I couldn't hear anything except his voice. I was so happy and so shocked that I didn't know what to say or do. But before I could give any response or reaction we were disturbed by his friend, Sohail. He arrived calling Hamza's name and started pulling him away saying "Come over here with me". Hamza said 'What? What is it?" But Sohail wasn't listening and said. "Don't ask what just come with I have some very important news for you. Come on, come with me now. I have been watching you for a while you can't do this now, so you had better come with me". He pulled Hamza's hand and took him away ooh I hate him.

Sohail was Hamza's friend he was a similar age and seemed to have the same business interests. Sometimes he would come for dinner with Hamza. I never liked him; he was always the bone in the roast' (translation of an Urdu proverb).

My heart was dancing and I felt like some one had presented me with whole world. Before leaving Hamza had given me some documents. I thought perhaps they would be love letter but it was better than that. They were my admission letters from the college. I was so glad and exited. I went to bride room and put those documents in my bag to make sure they would be safe and then I went back and joined the party. I danced with my friends; Hosai, Ogai, Neelam and the others.

Hamza suddenly seemed to be the super man in my life he had come in like a wind and blown away all my troubles.

Earlier that evening before leaving Hamza went on stage and gave two gifts to Imran. The next day we went to Islamabad Air Port and Imran left for Dubai. Dua came with us to the airport. She was crying a lot; my sweet Dua.

I was so worried about Hamza going away. After what he had said the night before; I wanted a chance to talk to him and tell him about my feelings; but he was gone. I kept trying his number but no one picked up the phone. Oh My All Mighty Allah what should I do?

I didn't know than that my distress would remain for a long time. All the way from Islamabad to Mansehra I kept dialing his number it was ringing but no one was picking how annoying was that.

When we got home, the first thing I did was to go and look at the documents Hamza had given me. The first letter was a conditional offer from the college, the second was an unconditional offer and the third letter said that I have paid three thousand pounds to the college. Hamza was a very rich man, he had a house in almost every big city and certainly in Pakistan Karachi, Peshawar etc. He also had two houses in Dubai and one in the United Kingdom. For such a person paying my fees was not difficult. His parents were not particularly rich; he was a self made man. But I was not concerned about his money at all. Once when we were talking together he said "Ayesha, don't you wonder where this money come from? Don't you feel afraid of me?" At first I was shocked but my heart would not allow me to think anything negative about him. So I said, "Why should I be afraid of you? Are you a monster?" He says "Maybe I am a monster. What then?" I said "Well in that case I would be lucky to have a monster- friend. No one else in the whole world has one." Of course I thought he was joking as usual. There were lots of strange things about his behavior but I never focused on them because I was blindly in love with him.

Imran call us from Dubai to let us know he had arrived safely. We were all very glad to hear from him.

Now that Hamza was arranging for me to go to the United Kingdom for my education I needed to have my IELTS test. I went to Islamabad with my Mom to take the test. Then I had to wait fifteen days for the result. Meanwhile I started to prepare my bank statement. My Dad's friend helped with this. We didn't have enough money in the bank to pay my fees, but I thought, since my fees had already been paid, this wouldn't matter. My passport was ready because I and Imran applied for our passports together from afghan consulate I still remember that hot summer day in Peshawar.

I SAID, "IMRAN". HE REPLIED with irritably "What?" I said, "It is so hot here, I don't like it". Imran said "Oh really Princess, Your Highness, I do apologize, I should have brought a mobile air conditioner with me to keep you cool". I said, with attitude, "Yeah definitely". Then Imran replied "Definitely my foot! Now shut up I am also sick of this heat; but don't worry we'll have the passport soon. It must be our turn next let's go. He asked before entering the room "May we come in Sir?" We heard a man's voice say "Yeah sure".

"Salaam (Peace), Sir". Salaam the officer said, "Your passport please" Imran hand him the passport he examined it and said "Hmmm one visit passport and one study passport, interesting". Imran explained "Actually, Sir I am going to Dubai for a visit and business and my sister wants to go to the United Kingdom for study". The officer signed and stamped the passport then said "Well best of luck. But, Miss have you

had your certificates attested?" I said "No, but I have brought my certificates with me. Here they are, can you attest them?" The officer looked at my certificates and then, with a smile said "Ms. Ayesha we can't attest it like this, first you need to have them attested by Pakistan's foreign office as you have studied in a Pakistani institution. Here is your passport". We thanked him and left the room saying "¹Khuda Hafis" (¹God bless you). Imran and I headed to the Pakistan foreign office by taxi. When we reached there I stepped forward to talk to the officer there I said: "Salaam Sir, here are my certificates please can you attest them I want to go abroad for my higher education." He looked at my certificates and gave a strange smile and said "Madam, first you need to have them attested by the Peshawar ministry of education, then you can bring them here". I was becoming very frustrated. But we got into a taxi and went to the education office. I handed my certificates for attestation to the education officer. He too smiled in a strange way and said "Madam, first you need to have your documents attested by the Abbottabad board and then we will attest them for you. Allah Hafis". I returned to Imran with sad and confused face. He asked: "What? What's happened now?" I said "I am hungry". Imran said "Ok my princess let's go". I told what had just happened after lunch. He was angry having had to accompany me back and forth all day long. Imran says: "That's it for me now. We are going back home. Next time you can come with Maa to get your papers attested".

"Ayesha!" Once again my Maa's voice brought me out of my memories. My God I really miss my brother. I hope he is ok; we haven't had any news from him after the first call. Everybody was worried about him and Dua was angry with him because he hadn't contacted her. But we thought and hoped he was just busy. Mother call me again, "Ayesha! Come here my dear, there is a call for you." I picked up the phone "Hello." A man said "Hello Ms. Ayesha. I want to tell you something. Don't get involved with Hamza, he is engaged to someone else". I said angrily "What? Who the hell are you?" He said "I am a well wisher" and the phone line went dead. I was very shocked and angry but I didn't believe him of course because I trusted Hamza even more than myself. So I turned a deaf ear to the call and went back to my room to say my prayer. After my prayers I stood before the mirror smiling thinking what a lovely thing it was to be in love. In love thoughts can take you to all sorts of different locations. When you fall in love you love music; I like every song now, I love colour everything seems so beautiful, when you are in love you start living in the world of love. You're environment can be exactly the same but everything is different because you are in love. If you have been in love you will know what I'm talking about. I trusted Hamza a lot but he had done so many strange things like not bringing his family to Imran's engagement. He told me that his family had been out of town. Once he told me about his old girlfriend, but I told him "I don't care about your past. Everybody has a past in their life," but nevertheless I was impressed by his honesty. The next night; I was sleeping and my mobile rung. I woke up and answered. A guy said "Hello darling, I am your lover. Would you like to be my friend? I heard your brother is out of the country." I was furious, I said "Shut up" and hung up. I turned my mobile off. It was 2:00 am. That night I couldn't sleep because I was wondering about the call, I was getting more and more calls like that and was getting used to keeping my phone in silent mod.

Chapter 5

It was the day before I had to leave for Islamabad for my appointment to have my TB test. IELTS test, bank statement, admission documents. Everything was ready. So I went to apply for my United Kingdom student visa. When I submitted my documents they told me to come back after three days for the biometrics. Wow! What a day it was! I went to the convention centre with Maa where I bought a ticket and caught the bus. The bus stopped in several different embassies: China, India, France and finally the United Kingdom embassy. I went in for the biometrics, wondering what other embassies I might have arrived at if I had stayed on the bus. How lovely it would be if the entire world would become one peaceful state with the same currency with, no war, no violence, and no boundaries and you could just ride a bus from one to the other like this. Anyway I was told that the embassy would take fifteen working days to respond to my application.

My friend Neelam came to our house, I was glad to see her and I said. "Salaam Neelam how are you my dear?"

she said "I am fine". Then I asked her "And tell me how is your love story?" she replied disappointedly "Don't ask. It's slower than a tortoise". She really is a very funny girl. Suddenly my mobile vibrated and I picked up and said 'Hello?' he said "Hi who is this?" I said "Don't be stupid - you must know whose number you have dialed and if you really don't know, why did you call?" The voice said "you might not know me but I know you very well so will you become my girl friend". That was the limit. I was really irritated. I replied with anger "Well if you know me you should also know that I'm from Afghanistan and if you tease me it's just one phone call to Afghanistan and someone will come and finish you off". The line went dead ***. Neelam said "Wow Ayesha, are you that dangerous?" Ayesha said "No I don't know anyone and here No one knows anything about the history or people of Afghanistan. But thirty years of war had created a horrible image in the minds of people here so I'm just using that image to get rid of these stupid callers; I really wish I could change the horrible image of Afghanistan and show people the real culture of my country but for now I am taking advantage of that image and guess what? It always works. Hahaha silly guys, you'll see he will not call again." But at that moment my cell starts vibrating again. Neelam laughed. I picked up said angrily "Hello." An educated sounding man replied, "Hello may I speak with Ms. Ayesha please?" I changed my tone and said politely "Yes, speaking". He said "Ms Ayesha, your passport is ready. Come and collect it tomorrow at 12:00am in the FedEx office." I was so pleased "Really? Thank you. Bye".

I said quickly. "Neelam give me a hug" I said. She was

surprised and asked "But what has happened?" I replied while jumping up and down in excitement "Buddy, my passport is ready". She says "Oh! Best of luck then".

The next day I went to Islamabad to collect my passport. I was so excited. I had that once I got my Visa the first person I would call would be Hamza. He would be so happy to hear my news. Inside the center there was a big picture of an Airplane, I gazed at the picture and said to myself "Hey Airplane soon I will be sitting in you." And then suddenly they called my number and I went to collect my passport. I checked all the pages but I could find no visa anywhere. Suddenly my forehead started sweating I was panicking and I asked the officer "Where is my visa?" He replied "Madam, open the other envelop. If the visa is not in your passport the details will be in this envelop." My All Mighty Allah, it wasn't my visa detail it was more like an order saying that I should be punished with execution by hanging. The documents in the envelope said that my visa application had been refused as the college I was enrolling at was not registered, and that my funds in the bank are not great enough to pay for my further education. The documents also told me that I would have a chance to appeal against the decision.

I felt like I was about to lose consciousness, the whole world was revolving around me.

The war and everything that happened to me affected me psychologically. Now, whenever I came across any unanticipated situation that I can't deal with I just lose consciousness. My Maa's voice shocked me to attentions "Ayesha what happened? Will you please tell me what happened?" I said "Maa I couldn't get my visa". I hugged her and cried, but` I also tried to keep control of myself because we were still in the middle of the centre, my blood pressure was dropping and I began to feel so defeated that I felt sure I would never achieve my dreams. We started our journey home. Islamabad was three hours away from Mansehra. All the way home I kept thinking, "Where is Hamza now? Why did he enrol me at an unregistered college? Why did he lie?" But there were no answer. I was so disappointed. Two weeks passed and still there was no news from my brother; my tears had dried but my questions were still gnawing at me. I had never forced Hamza to help me, so why did he promise to help, why did he take charge if he was incapable of helping? Where is he now?

No answer came. The days passed, Thursday arrived, I had completed my praying. A vehicle stopped outside our house and the doorbell rang. I answered; it was Hamza. I was so shocked that I could not speak a word. He entered the house; Maa saw him and immediately asked him, "Where is Imran?" He did not answer but instead dialed a number handed Maa the cell. Maa was confused but then she talked in the cell and found it was Imran she was so glad there were tears in her eyes and smile on face she talked to him for about five minutes. After the call ended I asked Hamza to give me Imran's number he said "Ok note it down... 001" I interrupted "001? That's not the code for Dubai, that's Canada's code". He said "Yes, you are right. You're a smart girl. This is Canada's code because Imran is in Canada". I said "What?" he replied "Yes Now note down the rest of the number" I wrote it down and said "Done", Hamza said "Ok, bye now, I have to go". I said "Why? Stay. Where are you going?" He said, "I have to leave. I have very urgent work to do. Goodbye". And with that he left.

Chapter 6

We were so glad to here from Imran. I quickly dialed his number and said "Salaam bro?" Imran said "Salaam my Princess. How are you?" I say "I am fine but how are you Mr. Columbus, I thought you were going to Dubai but you've ended up in Canada?" he said "Sis it's quite a long story, I will tell you some other time. But what about you, are you going to the United Kingdom?" I said sadly "Bro I lost the case, I can't get a visa". But he sounded pleased and said "Hmmmm that's great". I was so surprised Imran said "Hey don't get me wrong, I will pray that you get your visa and make your dream of studying abroad come true. In fact I have been trying to help you, I have visited three universities here, you can visit their web sites I will mail the addresses and then you can choose the university you like best and send them your documents. I will trust your choice because you're a smart girl and then I will pay your fees. I can sort out all the documents and sponsor. But listen, I need you to remember one thing. Don't ever accept any help from

Hamz and don't contact him, ok? Anyway, Princess I have to go now, talk to you later, take care, bye".

After that Maa called Dad and gave him Imran's news and I spoke to Dua and gave her Imran's number.

Talking with Imran made me very confused. I went to my bedroom and dialed Hamza's number. I said "Hi yaar, how are you? Where have you been all this time?" He said "I am fine, baby, but where I have been is a long story. I will tell you if you come and meet me on your own someday". I was very surprised "What?" I said. Then he said "Well, think about it. Anyway what's going on with your visa?" I said "I can't get the visa". He said "Don't worry, it's ok, we will try again. But I have another idea for you. Why don't you marry me and we can go to Dubai and settle down." I said "Hmm… what?!" and he said "Yeah, well think about that too". Then after a pause he said "Well baby, we've been talking for thirty minutes now. Enough for today, I will call you tomorrow. Bye. Bye" After he put the phone down I was angry and I thought to myself "Enough for today my foot, I always hate it when he says "Enough for today" as if it's a dose of medicine and not a phone call.

Why was everybody behaving so strangely? Everything seemed to be so complicated. What was going on? I needed to find out. I was lost in my thoughts again. What is it that he wants to tell me that he wants us to meet alone? I will go and meet him but I can't understand why he wants me to go alone; he's never asked for that before; why has he asked me to move to Dubai? If he really loves me and wants to marry me why doesn't he bring his parents to my house and ask my parents for my hand.

That's what happened with Dua, and with Seema, that's what all true lovers do. I've never gone to meet someone on my own before. At college my friends said that it was wrong, that bad girls go to meet guys alone. Why doesn't he want us to be lawfully married if he wants us to have a relationship why, why? I was crying helplessly then suddenly the phone rang, I picked up and said. "Hello." It was a man's voice that said "Hello Ms. Ayesha this is your well-wisher I want to tell you that Hamza is black listed from the United Kingdom. He can never go back there. He is also engaged to another girl. You can find out more about him by going to his house. Write down the address". I wrote down the address and asked "Who are you? How do you know all this?" But the call went dead. I look at his address, my hands were shaking. My All Mighty Allah, finally his address is in my hands, I have to go there; if All Mighty Allah has sent this address to me; he must mean something special by it. I must not miss this chance; I will go to his house and see what happens. I called Neelam and she arrived in three hours. I said "Salaam, Neelam," she replied "Salaam my dear, what's up? You seem quite happy what's happened." I said anxiously, "I have got his address and I want to go there". She said "Really. Wow. Ok when you do want to go?" I said "Tonight". But she said "No dear, tonight is not possible for me, let's say tomorrow night at 3:00am." I said "Ok, done." She said "That is the best time to go because my Maa and Papa are going to Lahore for a marriage and my two cousins are staying with me to look after me. I will put sleeping pills in their milk and then I will miscall you and then we can leave. I too want to find out about your Hamza. See you tomorrow at 3:00 am. Bye". Oh my All Mighty Allah, I was breathless thinking about him.

Chapter 7

That evening Dad came home with sweets, cold drinks and roast, he was so happy that we had heard from Imran, we had a little party and called Imran on the phone. After everybody had talked to him I got the phone and said "Hi bro what's up, man?" he said "I am fine my Princess, but my sweetheart I am so worried about you and I want to tell you some truths for your own good. Please try to listen with your mind not your heart, ok?" I said, "Ok, tell me, don't leave me in suspense.' He said "Ayesha, do you remember when I reached Dubai and called you guys from the airport". I said "Yeah". He continued "After I finished the call I was damn excited but when I turned round some cops took me to another room. They had my bag and they were asking, "Is this your bag?" I said, "Yes, why what's happened?" They said "Shut up and don't speak unless you are asked to." I was so scared. He took my jacket out and said "Is this yours". I was frightened now, I replied "Yes Sir". Then he took out the gift box and took out the drugs and asked "Is this yours?" I said "No". Then he got really angry and he said "if this bag is yours and this jacket is yours then this is all yours and we can arrest you." If you remember, on the night of my engagement *Hamza gave me two gifts and he said "This one is yours and this second gift is for my Aunt. When you reach Dubai I will call you and tell you the delivery address. I'm sure I don't need to say this to you but please don't open it, it's confidential."* Sis, over the last month I have been through hell. It was all caused by Hamza. He is a smuggler. But he didn't leave me alone, he spent loads of money and somehow he got me out of prison and he made me a fake passport which I used to get to Canada and now my new name is Haris, so whenever you call here tell them you want to talk to Haris. I'm doing pretty well now and I'm telling you this now but I don't want to discuss again, so you remember, but don't tell any one else, ok? I told you the whole secret. That's because now I am so away from you that will have to be Imran for yourself and protect yourself. The other reason that I'm telling is that I know that you love him." All through this his call I was speechless and tears were falling from my eyes and suddenly after hearing his last sentence I was shocked into alertness. The sound "haan?" came out of my mouth. Imran said "My Princess, no needs to be shocked, I know you better than any one. I know that you love him and that's why I am so worried about you. He doesn't deserve you, but I know you love him and I want to tell you that whatever decision you make I will be there for you as you have been for me and I will also talk with Dad. Hey are you still there?" I said "What? Yes, no, I mean yeah" then Imran says "Ok, now give the phone to Dad I want to talk with him." I gave the phone to Dad and ran out of the room. The next morning Dad called me to see him. I looked into his eyes; it was clear that he did not slept the whole night. I was scared, he said "Ayesha!" I replied "Yes, Dad". He continued "Last night I talked with Imran, he told me everything. Listen my daughter the things I have heard and the things I know about Hamza don't allow me to make any decision; but for me your happiness is more important than anything in this world. Now you are grown up girl, you are twenty years old and you can make decisions about your life yourself. I do not want to influence. When you were small things were different and we had to make decisions for you but now you are a grown up. Yes or no the decision will be yours and whatever it may be I will support you even against my family. I am putting a very big decision on your shoulders. The choice of your life. Be very careful and think a thousand times before you decide and remember that when you have made a decision I want you to explain your decision." I hugged my Dad and cried, his eyes were also wet then he left for work. My Dad had been a professor in Afghanistan he was a very nice and supportive man I knew he didn't like Hamza but he allowed me a choice anyway. After Dad left I talked to Hamza on the phone. I said "Hey Hamza, you know some days back someone called me and told me that you are engaged. Is that true?" He said "Who called you and when?" I said "Well he didn't tell me his name and I don't know anything about him. Now tell me are you engaged?" He said in a serious tone "Look Ayesha I have already told you that there were some ladies in my life before. Now I have to choose from two. I love you but she loves me. I am confused". On hearing this I became really angry and said "Ok, Hamza I have some important work to do, I will call you later bye." I was so angry. What does he think of himself?

The time was passing and I was counting every minute. At 11:00 pm everybody went to sleep. I got everything ready, at 2:45 am my cell vibrated, very punctual girl. Neelam had brought the car. She was a good driver in half an hour we were in Abbottabad. The address was easy to find and soon we were outside Hamza's house. I managed to get inside the gates by bribing the watchman. Looking in at the window I could easily see inside the house; there was party going on lots of people were there. How strange that he didn't invite us. Boys, girls, drinks and snakes there was everything! I saw him exchanged a black bag with someone.

Behind me was a car parking area. I saw some people coming out of the house and towards the car park. In order to hide I ran into a small out house. I heard a car leaving. No one was in the out house, it was dark, somehow I found the switch and turned the light on I was amazed by what I saw. Oh my All Mighty Allah; a huge picture of me on the wall before me. I looked all around on all the walls were poems and pictures of me in different poses. Oh wow! And I looked beautiful. I never thought Hamza would be this romantic. Shooo shweet (so sweet). I felt glad to choose him as my life partner. Now I realized why he always asked for my photos whenever we were online. After seeing the room I thought that everything was clear. I was so happy thinking that he must love me so much. So I decided I should be with him and that it doesn't matter whatever he did because life is so short and from that moment onward I wanted to spend all my life with my love. And I hoped that my love for him would bring him to a new and better path. Thinking these lovely thoughts I turned to go back home but at that moment oh my God everything vanished. I felt like I would lose consciousness but I managed to control myself. I had seen another picture; it was a huge picture of Hamza's engagement to an African girl. I didn't think she was as pretty as me. But my heart was broken. At that moment Neelam gave me a missed call and my cell vibration reminded me where I was. I turned the light off and rushed out of the building. I saw a vehicle stopping in the yard and a girl stepped out of it. Shit, it was the African from the picture. Hamza came out to meet her and then they went into the house together. I made a dash to Neelam car and she drove us away. How similar that thing was with our lives she got in and I got out of Hamza's life.

Chapter 8

"Hamza control yourself you looked like you were about to fall to the ground." Hamza said "Monica, Sohail just leave me alone I am fine" Monica said "No, you are not well, look at yourself, what's happened?" Hamza said: "Don't touch me, I said, I am fine. Leave me". Monica replied irritably "Fine!" and left. Sohail came towards Hamza and said "What is the matter. This all happening according your own plan; I told you it would be tough leaving your love is not an easy thing. I warned you but you still kept making me call Ayesha. And now she is out of your life forever. Happy?" Hamza hugged Sohail and burst into tears. After a while he managed to control himself. Sohail offer him some water and after having a glass of water he said. "I am fine now. And I am happy that it is all over now." Sohail asked "But why? Why don't you just marry her and live a happy life" Hamza said "in this life I don't think I deserve her. I can't marry her; I can't tell her the truth about my life because then I will be a criminal in her eyes where I was once a hero. I know she will never marry me when she knows the truth my reality so it's better that it is all settled this way. I think this is the punishment for all my evil deeds: to lose the most precious girl – the love of my life. This is my punishment I have to accept it. This world is truly round in every sense: it revolves your deeds come back to you. She was my Darling, my sweetheart, my Princess, my love and will always be the wind of fresh air".

I told Neelam everything. She kept driving and soon we were well clear of the area. When we reached Mansehra Neelam stopped the car. I hugged her and cried. My heart was broken, I felt like someone had taken out my life. I have always been so proud of myself and my beauty I never thought that I will lose my love to another woman. I hate her, I hate her. After that visit everything was clear to me. I decided to move out of Hamza's life forever. It was tough, the decision was killing me, but I had no other choice really, my mind knew I had made the right decision. When I got back home it was 5:00 am Neelam dropped me home and left. I went quietly to my bed, removed the pillows that were sleeping in my place and put my face in one pillow and cried until I fell asleep. As it was Sunday I woke up late and Papa had already gone to the shop. I was determined to tell him my decision in the evening. I started to work on the computer. I visited different websites and filled in online forms for different universities and finally I checked my email. My God there was mail from Hamza's, but now I had made my decision his mail was not important. I opened the mail it said "Ayesha, I have thought a lot. You are a nice girl but I am going to marry someone else. It is true that I am engaged but I never told you because I loved you. But you want to go to the United Kingdom whereas she is ready to spend her life with me in Dubai and she know everything about me where as you don't know very much about me. I am not sure what your reaction will when you find out the truth about me. You are a nice and beautiful girl and I am sure you will find your Mr. Right soon. I am sorry but I can't tell you my truth. Please forgive me for bothering you this long".

He doesn't know that Imran has told me about him. But it doesn't matter now. I don't need to tell him anything. He has already locked all the doors. I read the mail again and got so angry I sent him one back. "Mr. Hamza you are right. I am just too good for you and I am a nice girl and I will find someone else because I deserve better than you and my Superman will come one day for me. I was wrong about you", after sending this mail I switched off the computer. I couldn't control myself this time. Darkness come before my eyes and I don't know what happened after that but when I opened my eyes I was in hospital I tried to get up but Ouch! There was drips in my hand Maa and Dad were near me, the lights were on it seemed to be evening. I asked "Maa what's going on?"

She said, "How are you, my dear? We brought you in emergency. Your blood pressure was low and you had °105 degree temperature. Doctor arrives checks the report and asks me how you are Miss? I reply "I am fine thank you". He says to my parents you can take her home now try not to stress her and give these medicines for two days she will be fine but if blood pressure drops again bring her here.

The next day I said "Papa, I have made my decision I will not marry Hamza." Dad was so glad he hugged me and said "I am proud of you my dear I was expecting such an answer from you. Now explain your answer." I said, "Dad I found out the truth about him and I can't marry him. I have realized that my life partner should be someone whom I have known from my childhood someone the family knows and who's family we know and someone my own age." Dad said "Wow, my dear, your decision has made me very happy. Now you must rest".

Chapter 9

One month passed and Ayesha was still in depression. She has forgotten what it was to laugh.

The doorbell rang and Maa opened the door to Neelam who said "Salaam dear aunt." Maa said "Salaam dear thank you for coming at my request". Neelam said "Don't worry about that Aunty it's my duty, I wanted to come earlier but I went away to Karachi for a month, anyway, how is Ayesha?" Maa said "My dear, I'm afraid Ayesha is not good. That jolly girl who was so full of life has now forgotten what it is to live, and to laugh. She is like the living dead we did everything we could think of to bring her back to life but nothing has helped. It's like she doesn't want to live. I am scared and that's why I called you here, to see if you can do anything". Neelam said "its ok Aunty don't cry, I will talk with her, where is she?" Maa said "In her room". Neelam went to her room and shouted: "Booo gotcha. Hey! You didn't jump." Ayesha said "Salaam Neelam," She replied "Salaam Ayesha, how are you, pretty lady". Ayesha said "Fine". Neelam said in surprise "Just fine? What's up buddy? Ayesha used to tell you a whole story using all her energy and now you are just fine? What's happened to you?" Ayesha said, "Nothing". Neelam said "What do you mean nothing huh? What are you doing to yourself? Are you alive? Do you have any idea how upset your parents are about your condition? Why you are doing this? This sadness, lifelessness, just look at your face. Do you even recognize yourself in the mirror? Where is my bubbly friend? Just forgive him and forget him." Ayesha said with anger "Forgive him. No Neelam no, I can never forgive him, he is a villain, a man who killed his love with his own hands, he killed me, he killed my love". Neelam said, "Ayesha, maybe he had some problem that meant that he couldn't accept you. He made money in so many wrong ways that he probably thought that he didn't deserve an innocent girl like you." Ayesha said, "Problem my foot if he had a problem he had no right to fall in love. If he was committed to someone else why did he come into my life? You are right that his money came between us, it's very true that excess of anything is bad and it's not true that money brings happiness: money brings distraction, money took away my love. Now I hate him. I hate him because I loved him so much". After saying all this she started crying and Neelam hugged her and said "Oh my dear don't cry. He doesn't deserve you." But Ayesha kept crying. Then Neelam said "Ok, cry as much as you can and finish this once and for all."

After crying Ayesha did feel better. Neelam said "Now get ready we are going to Deemas (name of shopping mall) there is a new sale on, I have brought the car, let's go shopping. Come on now, give me a smile." Ayesha gave a reluctant smile, Neelam said "There's a good girl. Dua is on her way to join us too". The doorbell rang. Neelam said "That must be her. I'll go get her." Dua arrived and said, "Salaam Ayesha." "Salaam Dua." Said Ayesha. Dua said "Oh my God what a pretty smile, here I've brought a gift for you". Ayesha opens the gift it was a very nicely stitched top she says "Thanks a lot yaar (buddy)". Dua said "No need for thanks and no need for sorry in a friendship. Now put it on and let's go".

After some weeks of struggling; Ayesha was out her depression. Her parents were very happy and her brother Imran called her every day.

Always our lives are in motion. We should not stop living because of hardships. Happiness and sadness are the two colours of life without which life is colourless. So I made an oath to myself: "I will continue living. I will live my life with full spirit; it doesn't mean that I don't love him anymore or that I have forgotten what he put me through. It's just that I also love myself and I have to live for my family. The bend in the road is not the end of road unless you fail to make the turn. And I hope this road will take me to some nice place or at least to somewhere new."

In the evening I was reading a book when Dad came to my room and said, "My doll I am very happy that you have accepted your situation and are out of your depression. Today I want to tell you something. Do you remember the words you said when you explained your decision?" I said "Yes, I remember." Father said, "I have such a proposal, but I have been delaying your Aunt Meena. She has asked for your hand for her son,

Umer. Now I would like to know your opinion on this proposal?" I said "As you wish Papa". He said "All Mighty Allah bless you, I will call them now". Papa kissed my forehead and left the room. Aunt Meena fixed the date of next Monday for the engagement. Maa and Paa informed Dua, Imran and the rest of our relatives.

I was not happy nor I was sad, I was quiet and I left everything on All Mighty Allah. My condition was critical and I needed support desperately and thinking of Umer became that support it made me a bit more relaxed. He fitted completely the conditions I had mentioned to my father. Maa looked after all the preparations. Dua and Neelam helped out a lot. Everybody was so happy and excited and I was glad to see everyone happy and satisfied. Umer's arrived with great pomp and show. They brought three well decorated trays of gifts and everyone went in the guest room; after seeing all this I became so happy and I thought my engagement would be a great shock for Hamza. I said to myself "Yahoo! Mr. Hamza, now you will realize how awful it is to see your love with someone else." I was so looking forward to seeing Hamza jealous.

Dua arrived to take Ayesha into the other room. Ayesha wore a peach colour dress, she wore a little makeup and she looked great. When she came into the room her Aunt welcomed her hugging her and kissing her forehead and then she made her sit beside her. Umer looked quite smart; he was a very handsome guy. Everyone was so happy. Then Umer said "dear Uncle if you don't mind I want to talk with Ayesha alone". Her father agreed and they both went to the other room. Ayesha started to get nervous.

Umer said "Ayesha you are a very beautiful girl and any man on this earth would be lucky to have a lovely girl like you in his life". Ayesha remained silent, she was looking down, but she smiled. Umer continued, "But I am afraid to say that I am not that lucky guy. May All Mighty Allah bless you and I know you will find your Mr. Perfect soon but it's not me. I loved a girl at college, I told my family about her but they did not approve. Everyone wanted me to marry you. They rejected the girl whom I wanted to marry and she is engaged to someone else. Now I have a plan: to punish my family I will refuse this proposal but next month I will come back with my parents and marry you." Ayesha was burning with anger, finally she burst out and said "Mr. Umer you want to punish your family but I don't want to be punished for the rest of my life by marrying a guy like you. Just get lost".

She went straight to the other room where everyone were sitting and enjoying tea. When she entered the room; everyone looked at her with hopeful eyes. She told everyone about the things that Umer had told her and concluded: "Aunty, I am sorry but I will not marry your son". After this decision her aunt and all other guest left gossiping. Ayesha hugged her parents and cried. Her Dad said "Well done Ayesha I am pleased with your decision, now please stop crying." Her mother said "I am also proud of you my dear." Her parents' words gave her strength. But she was also angry that second formula for finding a life partner had failed. She decided she had better just leave everything to destiny because one never knows what is going to happen. After that she continued going to her job and life returned to its normal routine. The time flew.

And now her brother had been living in Canada for about two years.

One day Ayesha was sitting before mirror and talking with All Mighty Allah. "Why me, why me? All Mighty Allah All the time I try to make a ship of hope with broken tools but my journey has ended before it began; first Hamza left me and now this silly Umer. What next? What do have in store for me? What am I going to do now? Where should I go?" The door rang she opened the door and it was the TCS boy, he said "Ms. Ayesha Popal?" she replied "Yes" then he said "We have a letter for you, please sign here". After handing over the letter he left. She read "London Metropolitan University", then she remembered that she had filled in a form requesting a prospectus." The envelope contained a CD and an admission form. She watched the CD on her computer and was very impressed; it was the University of her Dreams. She grabbed a pen to start filling in the form and at that moment the phone rang.

She said "Hello!" and Imran replied "Hi Princess, how are you?" She said "I am fine, what's up?" Imran said "Listen carefully, last week I have sent the forms and documents for you, Dua, Mom and Dad. Since the day I arrived here I have been trying to get you all here. My lawyer has had your case put forward by twelve months. Next month you will get some forms and instructions. Follow them. Since you are a student they will try to handle your case earlier. Don't worry. You also need to go to Islamabad for some medical tests. In fifteen days I am coming back for the wedding". Ayesha said "Ok" he said "Ok take care; I've got to go now, Allah Hafiz."

The next day the postman delivered the documents. Ayesha got really confused trying to decide between Canada and London Metropolitan University but since her whole family was going to Canada she decided to go with them.

They got everything prepared for the wedding. Imran comes back from Canada and one month after his marriage they all went to Canada with Canadian immigration visas.

Ayesha started going to a Canadian university. Her dreams had come true after all and she was so happy.

Life in Canada is quite stylish, posh and easy. You feel complete freedom to do anything you want. There were also massive cultural differences to get used to, like the concept of unmarried couples etc.

I visited a museum where security checks your bag. In Asia they check your bag too, but the difference is that here they check to see if there is a knife or sharp object whereas in Asia they check your bag to see if there is a bomb. I made some very good friends and life was going well, but deep inside I knew that something was wrong. One day I was sitting in the cafeteria having a coffee and I noticed a couple. And that got me thinking about Hamza. All those raw memories started revolving in my mind and I got so upset I left the cafeteria and started walking out. Nearby there was a park, I was moving quickly as usual and then, suddenly from behind two hands came out. One grabbed my mouth and one caught my arm and pulled me. I was terrified and when I turned round I was surprised to see Hamza standing before me. Without thinking I just hugged him and started crying he was also crying. That feeling was so special that I hoped it would last forever. Then after a while he said, "I am married now." I felt like someone had thrown hot water over me and all of a sudden he become a stranger to me I pushed him away and said "Then what the hell are you doing here?" he said "I just came to meet you and tell you to move forward with your life and never look back." I said "Oh really, wow, but I don't need your advice!" I could not bear to be with him anymore I turned and started running furiously forgetting about my surroundings, tears streaming down my face as I crossed the road. I didn't listen to the car horns and suddenly I saw a car coming full speed towards me. I was frozen to the spot, my mind stopped working, the vehicle was coming fast, all I could hear was terrible noise and a shout and then there was darkness.

A guy stepped down from the vehicle and said, "Damn, I hope the girl is ok" a crowd had gathered. The guy said, "it's ok I am a doctor I will take her to the hospital". A man in the crowd said "Mister it's not that straightforward. You should wait for the police before you do anything." The guy said "Alright then I will stay here but I want to inform you that the girl is in shock and you should let me take her to hospital. If I don't she could slip into a coma, do you want to be responsible for that?" The bystander looked like he was loosing his nerve and the rest of the crowd fell silent. So the driver took Ayesha into his car and drove away.

The driver said to himself: "Coma my foot, my car has barely touched her. I don't know why she is pretending, but thank God I managed to get rid of that crowd. Allah why did you make women? They are at the route of every problem. Today I needed to get going early and now thanks to this damn accident I will be late. Listen girl, enough of this drama, you are not hurt you'd better get up because you cannot fool me, I am really a Doctor". There was no response. "What should I do now? I'd better check the girl again and make sure she is ok. First I should call Allen. "Hi Allen, listen just handle everything and fill out an emergency form, I need a half day leave because I will not be able to come in." Allen said "Ok but what's happened? You sound upset." Elham said "Nothing special just a minor accident, now I am opening the car door to check the girl. I know she would be fine… but there was no response from ….. Allen said "Why have you stopped taking?" Dr.Elham said "Nothing - just this girl- I will call you later". He thought, 'Wow, she reminds me of sleeping beauty, I'll check her breath. She is breathing that means she's alive. Good pulse hmm her hand is so soft. What is happening? I feel like to hold this hand forever." Then his mind said "Dr.Elham Control yourself!" "Well the pulse is very low. I'll check for fever. Oh my God her forehead is burning, she has a high fever. That's why she is unconscious. Silly me. I thanked Allah. Good job she didn't hear else; what would she think of me? Wait a minute why do I care what a strange girl thinks of me. Never mind now what should I do now? I can't go to hospital. I think I should go home and give her a serum then she will be fine. But hospital… there would be ten thousand forms to fill in and lots of excuses and tests. As she has a fever I think it is best that I go home and take care of her.

When Ayesha opened her eyes she found herself in a well decorated room. She looked around. It was a big guest room decorated with blue and white colours and she was on the sofa. Then she turned her head to the right side and was shocked to see a guy sitting close to her. The guy was quietly saying to himself "what a pretty girl, what an innocent face". The sound was so low Ayesha couldn't understand what he was saying. She said. "What? Who are you? Where am I?" He stands up and responds "Hello Madam, I am Dr.Elham. I am not so very glad to meet you. You know that you have been sleeping for two hours you are a very lazy girl". She stared at him with angry eyes. He continued "Madam don't you know there are lots of ways to commit suicide without crushing yourself under the vehicle of a gentleman like me?" Ayesha said, 'what the hell?' but she spoke in Dari. The doctor said "Oh you are Afghan." She replied "Yes". Then he said "Don't you feel ashamed of yourself, trying to commit suicide and giving Afghans a bad name?" Now that was the limit, and Ayesha got very angry and said "Excuse me Mister. Will you please stop lecturing me?" He replied "Wow, great reward for saving your life".

Then Ayesha felt apologetic and said "Ok I'm sorry. Thanks very much for saving my life. I wasn't actually trying to kill myself. It was just an accident, I was in a state and I just found myself in the middle of the road in front of your vehicle".

The doorbell rang and the man stood up to answer it. The man was six feet tall handsome with a nice body and nicely trimmed hairs. When he opened the door an angry lady came in looking tired and angry. But she was a sweet looking old lady with a grey bob hair she was wearing a long skirt and a camel coloured shirt.

Dr Elham said "Salaam Maa". She replied "Salaam Elham! Now take these shopping bags". She was very tired and as she settled down she said, "Oh my All Mighty Allah, when will this man understand his responsibilities and get married and bring a wife into this house to take charge of things. When All Mighty Allah?"

The lady came and sat on the other couch opposite Ayesha. Ayesha gave a puzzled smile and said "Salaam Khala Jan" (Hello dear Aunt). But the lady ignored her and continued her complaints to All Mighty Allah. "See, All Mighty Allah, now I am so desperate that I see an illusion of an Afghan girl sitting on that sofa and talking with me. I am going mad".

But Elham said, "Maa this is not an illusion, this is really a girl". The lady was very surprised and said, "What? Really" He said "Yes Maa. She is my Friend". Ayesha says "Yes Aunt, I am Ayesha".

The lady said "I think today the Sun rose from the west! (Translation of Asian Proverb) Elham and a girl!" Before the discussion could go any further Ayesha stood up and said "Aunt, I am getting late, I have to leave now" and she began to leave. The aunty says "Wait my dear. Give me a hug and relax a while, Elham will drop you where you need to go. I won't let you go alone. Elham say you'll drop her later". He said "Ok Maa. Madam this way please".

She gave him her address and he drove home. When they got there she said loudly "Stop". He said "What happened?" she said "Nothing actually, this is my house."

She stepped out of vehicle and said "Thanks a lot Dr. Elham". He said "You can call me Elham". She said "Ok" and started to turn towards her home. He said "Excuse me madam, only a single thank you -no coffee, no tea?" Ayesha said "Oh sorry, please come in." He said "No Ayesha, then after a pause he asked "I can call you Ayesha?". She said "Yes Oh off course". He continued "I was just kidding anyway. Thanks for the hospitality but next time Inshallah (by the will of God). But one thing I should tell you- I lied to you." She asked "When?" He replied "I said I wasn't glad to meet you." She said "Yeah you did say that." He said "That was a lie. In fact I am very glad to meet you".

He put on his glasses and left. Ayesha returned to her house and her mother opened the door and said, "Salaam. Why you are late?" Ayesha said "I was with my friend Maa, so that's why." After saying that she rushed to her room. And started talking with herself: "Oh God I hate lying, but what can I do if I tell her about my accident she will be so worried. Oh I am so sleepy. I don't know what medicine that silly so- called doctor has given me, but I cannot stand any longer I am dying to sleep."

Chapter 10

One week passed and Ayesha's life returned to its normal routine. Although she had had quite a shock and now she wanted to make her busy in the household chores without thinking, like a machine. Life continued and Sunday arrived. That day they had a house cleaning program everyone was busy, changing curtains and sofas and rearranging the furniture. From the day they arrived they had wanted to change the house decoration but since every one was busy so they hadn't had time. At last on Sunday they were all available. After they had cleaned the house they all had baths and ordered pizza.

The pizza boy arrived and Imran shouted "Yahoo pizza and cold drinks!" Maa called "Everyone comes to the dining room." They had all gathered in the dining hall when the door bell rang again. Papa said "Oh who is it now?" Imran asked "Maa have you ordered more pizza?" She said "No I thought five would be enough for us". Imran said "Ayesha you open the door."

Ayesha opened the door and was very surprised to see

Elham's family. They greeted her and entered the house. She talked to herself quickly "Oh my God they have come to complain about my accident that day." Then Ayesha made a gesture to Dua so that she would understand who it was.

Elham's family were very impressed with the house decoration. Ayesha and Dua went to fetch tea. Elham's Mother introduced herself and his father told them about their family and his son. Ayesha's family was very happy to see Afghan people abroad.

In the kitchen Ayesha asked Dua "What should I do now? Why are they here? What if Elham tells them about that day? Oh My God". But she got angry because Dua was smiling and asked her "Now why you are smiling?" Dua said "I must say that guy is handsome and if they have come here then the matter is serious". Ayesha asked nervously "What do you mean serious?" Dua said, "Silly girl what do you think they came here for to complain about you or to praise our decoration?" Ayesha said, "Maybe!" Dua said "Maybe! Shut up. Now don't act stupid you can understand the meaning of someone coming like this; they are here to ask for your hand". Ayesha said "I don't think so". Dua said "We will see".

They both smiled and took the tea and snacks into the guest room. After serving the tea Dua sat beside Imran and by chance Ayesha sits with Elham.

Elham's mother said. "Sister I want to tell you clearly I love your daughter and I want to take her to my home as my daughter. See what a wonderful pair they make together as husband and wife?" His father said "now since you know everything about our family and we know about yours I am sure you will not have any doubts and if you still have any confusion about us, this is our complete address and all our contacts; you can cross verify everything!"

Ayesha's father replied "we have no problems but since this is the decision of Ayesha's life so, whatever she says will be our decision; Ayesha dear what do you think about all this?"

Ayesha remained quite but Elham said "Uncle if you don't mind can I have a word with Ayesha alone". Her father said "Sure, why not". Ayesha led Elham to the other room.

It reminded her of the day when she spoke to Umer in the separate room. She remembered how angry she had felt. Due to that bad thought she looked quite upset while Elham came close to her and said. "I love the taste of human flesh, roasted, I am a monster". After hearing this she gave a weird look to Elham. He said "Just kidding but you seem so scared of me so I thought I'd give it a try". She smiled; Elham said "Now that is what I call a million-dollar smile".

He then got down on bended knee and looked towards Ayesha and said "Madam Ayesha, the most beautiful girl I've ever come across, kindly accept this ring and grant me that I may live with you every moment of my life from here after?"

I was not expecting this from this silly doctor. What should I do? Better close my eyes and think. Then Hamza's words came into my mind "Ayesha go ahead with your life. I am married". Oh Allah, Hamza broke my heart but I do not have the guts to break someone else's. So I opened my eyes and said "Yes Elham, take my hand and put the ring on." Elham hugged me and we both returned to the other room He announced the decision. Everyone was very happy. They all ate sweets and then fixed the marriage date. Eventually Elham's family left, I felt so strange I just rushed to my room and prayed- please Allah tell me it's a dream and it's not reality please, and thinking that went to sleep.

The next day my mobile rang and woke me up at 9:00am. It was an unknown number. I answered: "Hello?" A boy replied "Good Morning sweetheart, get ready I will pick you at 10:00am then we will go shopping, see you bye". What? Aaaaaaaaaah my God! So it had not been a dream it had been reality and I couldn't believe it at all. A single word "yes" can change my life this much I didn't like it; enough now I will tell him I can't marry him and to leave me alone. I will feel no sympathy at all if people can break my heart why not me. That's it I have decided I am going to finish this today. First I will tell everyone at home and Elham when he comes to meet me, mom and dad can inform his parents. So with that spirit I got changed and went down stairs where everyone was happy and in the mood to tease me. And it was only 9:30 and Elham was already in our house having breakfast, I just can't believe this man he changed all my plans by coming this morning. Well I didn't said a single word to anyone, I had my breakfast quietly and went out. But they just thought I was shy.

Elham came and started driving the car I tried many times to tell him but every time he changed the subject. My God, he was so happy you could see it all over his face his eyes were sparkling with pleasure like he had conquered the world.

He said "Hey sweetheart where are you? I am talking with you". I looked at him and he continued "You know Ash?" I asked "Ash?" he said, "Yes Ash your nickname, sweet and beautiful like our love. Wow". "How Silly" I laughed, he said "Yeah that's my girl I know you must be thinking how silly this is but thanks to you I am not myself anymore I can't recognize myself, I am a changed person. Well here I will stop; this is the place where we will buy the dress. Let's go."

We were shopping and laughing all day. He had a very good sense of humor, he bought thousands of things for me and whenever I said no he said "Maa said; actually she also wanted to come shopping with us but I stopped her so your mom and my mom decided to meet up separately and decide the guest list but she asked me to buy all the things her daughter in law liked so let me fulfill that".

Actually it's an old saying in Afghanistan when they take the new bride for shopping to buy all the things that touch the hand of bride and this man really fulfilled that. He dropped me home that night.

"So Ash thanks for the beautiful day I had a wonderful time. I hope you did as well now it's time to say bye, I hope you'll miss me." I was holding the shopping bags; he came near and kissed my face then returned to his car, gave a wink and drove away.

The days were passing quickly everyone was very happy and finally I also accepted the decision of my destiny. Elham is a very nice human being and crazy about me. All that made me fall in love with him. He cares for me a lot and the feeling that in this big world of millions of people there is someone who is living for you and can die for your smile is such a beautiful feeling that it made me move forward in my life. Love definitely makes your life beautiful. Marriage is a big decision and the base should be love because you cannot spend your whole life with someone whom you don't love.

The next month the marriage came. Everything happened fantastically. Since the theme of the marriage was love, so the whole hall was decorated with red and white colours and red and white heart shaped balloons. The bride arrived first in a Green gown (as it was a custom of Afghans to wear a green gown before Nikkah) (Nikkah= the Muslim act of marriage where the bride and groom say I do, I do after hearing the holly verse) and after Nikkah the dinner is usually served to all the guests and after dinner the bride comes in with her white gown and the groom wears his black suit.

For their honeymoon they went to London and wow- what a city! It is truly the business and fashion capital, the heart of the world. Such a multicultural place you can see people from all over the world in London. We visited Harrods, Hyde Park, London Bridge, The London Eye, South Hall the Little India, Selfridges and many others. It's so big, it's so beautiful the people are so helpful; if you are in London alone carrying some heavy luggage don't you worry - there is a whole world to help you out. Because I like London so much I transferred my university credit hours here and Elham started working as a doctor in London instead and we lived together happily.

It's now two years that we are living in London and

today I am wearing my favourite dress sitting next to Dad and Elham and I am so excited obviously not because of my dress or position but because it's my graduation day and all my family is here with me they came all the way from Canada for the ceremony the announcer finally called my name I got my degree ooh I am so happy I came back hugged every one they were so happy for me later I saw Imran talking with Elham I went and knocked on his back with my degree he turned to me I said see I told you I will get my degree like this he kissed my forehead and said I am so proud of you my princess. See in life if you have a vision go for it and later on your greatest critic will automatically become your greatest admirer.

At last she did completed her studies and also found her Super Man or Mr. Perfect. This is the life we dream and struggle for. Although it's not important sometimes that we achieve exactly what we dreamed but we should not quit struggling because later or soon we do get our reward. So if our plans succeed we should be glad and if they don't we should be glad still, because in destiny God has a better plan for us.

Lightning Source UK Ltd.
Milton Keynes UK
30 December 2010

165040UK00001B/5/P